A HAT-TRICK

BY
ROB CHILDS

ILLUSTRATED BY
KARIN LITTLEWOOD

OF SPORTS STORIES

LONGMAN

Walk Tall

"Oh, no!" groaned one of the footballers. "Look who's coming."

"It's Stilts!" cried another, pretending to run off. "Watch out or you'll get trampled on. He won't be able to see us down here."

Stephen Jackson heard their laughter as he walked across the school playing field. He guessed it would be aimed at him, as usual... more of their silly jokes about his height.

He knew he should be used to it by now, but it still hurt. They just never gave up.

Jason, the school team soccer captain, was the first to greet him. "Spotted you a mile off, Stilts. You stand out like a lighthouse."

"Yeah!" cackled someone else. "What's the weather like up there?"

"Very funny," Stephen sneered. "I've only heard that fifty million times. OK, so I'm tall, why don't you leave off about it?"

"Tall , he says!" Jason mocked. "You're a freak, Stilts. You belong in a circus."

He tried to ignore the insult. Jason was not

somebody you picked a fight with.

"Look, can I play or not?" Stephen asked him.

"No chance. You're useless. You just stand around like a telegraph pole getting in the way. Go and play netball over there with the girls. If you're lucky, they might want to hang their net around your neck."

The others laughed and broke away to carry on with their lunchtime game, some barging deliberately into Stephen as they went past. Left on his own, he aimed an angry kick at a nearby stone – and missed. He nearly toppled over off-balance as his right foot swished through the air at nothing.

Tears sprang to his eyes but he didn't want anyone to see him cry. They'd taunt him even more then. "What if I *am* useless at football?" he muttered. "It still doesn't stop me wanting to play it."

Feeling sorry for himself, he didn't hear somebody come up quietly behind him.

"Take no notice of them," a voice said. "They're not worth it. Come and have a kickabout with me instead, if you like."

Stephen spent the next five minutes trying his very best to pass the white plastic football back within reach of his unexpected new friend. His efforts, however, were not a success.

He knew you should use the side of the foot, but somehow he just couldn't quite do it properly. Determined to get it right, he ran up to the ball once more and this time toe-ended it so hard that it sped way wide of its target like a stray, out-of-control missile.

Sanjay Patel shook his head and smiled. "Doesn't matter, I'll get it again – as long as you tell me something first. Why do they call you *Stilts?*"

Stephen didn't reply for a moment, then sighed. "If you must know, 'Stilts' is one of Jason's stupid nicknames for me. He keeps going on about how I should be in a circus."

"Circus?"

"Yeah, he reckons that when I'm wearing shorts, my thin legs stick out like those long wooden poles circus stilt-walkers balance on."

Sanjay chuckled. "I saw one of them on telly the other day. He was dead good, really clever. Never fell off once."

"Better than me, then. I was born clumsy. These are my own legs and I'm always falling over."

"Best to laugh it off," said Sanjay. "There's worse nicknames than Stilts."

"I know," said Stephen. "I get called most of them."

"Well, you know how that old saying goes. . . "

"*Sticks and stones may break my bones, but words will never hurt me*," they chanted together.

"Not true, of course," Stephen added, "but my big sister, Emily, always comes out with it when I moan to her about being bullied."

"You've got a *big* sister! She must be huge."

"Wait till you see her. She makes me look almost normal," he said, returning Sanjay's smile. "She had the same problems as me till she took up netball. It helps to be tall in that, I guess. As soon as she started winning games for the school team, the other girls suddenly got all pally."

"Same thing could happen for you then," Sanjay said. "Er... at football, I mean."

"Doubt it. You can see how brilliant I am. Look where that ball's gone."

"Hmm... perhaps you do need a bit of coaching first," Sanjay grinned, before running off to fetch it. He dribbled the ball back cleverly, twice flicking it up into the air and juggling it on both knees.

"Show-off!" Stephen cheeked him. "Now *you* answer a question – why are you wasting your time here with me instead of playing over there with them?"

"Simple. I don't like some of the names they call me, either," Sanjay said. "Especially behind my back, just loud enough for me to hear."

Stephen looked puzzled. "But you're in the school team. Nobody's more skilful than you with a ball. Are they jealous or something?"

"Maybe. But there's more to it than that."

"What do you mean?"

"Come off it. Even you must have noticed I'm not exactly the same colour as all the rest of them."

Stephen was shocked. "They get at you 'cos of that?"

"Yeah, well, that's how it goes," he said with a shrug. "People who are different in some way or other always seem to get picked on. Like you and me. Suppose we just have to put up with it."

"It's not right," Stephen said. "Wish there *was* something we could do about it. I'm sure fed up of them poking fun at my height."

"So why do you keep asking to join in their games? Even when they let you, it's only so they can run rings round you or knock you over."

Stephen nodded sadly. "I don't know why I bother, either. Guess I just like football, even if I'm not really built for it."

Sanjay stopped tapping the ball from one foot to the other. "What did you just say?"

"Er... I said something about being the wrong size to be any good at football."

"Oh, I don't know about that," Sanjay replied, beaming, looking Stephen slowly up and down. "You've gone and given me a wicked idea."

Without warning, he let out a whoop of excitement and booted the ball away high into the sky. "You're not the wrong size at all – in fact, you're just perfect!"

"Come on, jump!"

Every time Stephen tried to do what Sanjay wanted, he seemed to get his long legs in a terrible tangle and end up flat on his face.

They were in Stephen's back garden after school and Sanjay was throwing a ball into the air for him to jump up and head it back.

At least that was the idea. But Sanjay was starting to think that perhaps it wasn't a great one after all. Teaching Stephen how to head a ball properly was not proving as easy as he'd reckoned.

"It's no good, Sanjay. I'm hopeless, admit it. I just can't get the timing right. I either jump too soon and the ball hits me on the nose, or I jump too late and it sails over my head."

"Just got to keep at it, that's all," Sanjay said, determined not to give in. "You'll see. We'll show that lot at school how good it could be to have somebody really tall like you in a team who can head loads of goals. That'll shut them up."

"Huh! Fat chance," Stephen grumbled. "They always stick me right back in defence out of the way. And even when the ball does come near me, somebody makes sure they beat me to it."

They suddenly realised they were being watched. Emily, Stephen's older sister by two years, had come into the garden and Sanjay stared at her in amazement. She was a real beanpole, and he found himself just about level with her tummy.

"What are you two up to?" she laughed. "It looks like some strange new kind of dance, all that hopping up and down."

"I'm supposed to be jumping," Stephen said, pulling a face at her. "Just keep out of it, sis. I'm practising."

"What for, being a kangaroo?"

"I'm improving my heading, if you must know. Sanjay is helping me."

"Well, if you ask me, that's not the way to go

about doing it. It's like trying to throw the ball before you've caught it."

"Who's asking you?" Stephen snorted. "This isn't netball, you know. I'm not trying to catch it.'

"It looks to *me* like you are – in your mouth!"

Sanjay spoke for the first time to stop their argument. "I'll ask you, then. What are we doing wrong?"

"You're trying to do everything at once," Emily replied. "Stephen's got to learn how to jump properly first before he worries about having to head as well."

"Could you teach him? You know, show him how to outjump people, like you have to in netball."

"Sure. I'll be glad to. Just being tall isn't enough. You can't shoot if you don't get the ball."

"I'm not trying to shoot," sneered Stephen. "I want to head it."

"Same thing, different game, that's all," said Emily. "But I'll leave the heading bit to your soccer coach here."

Sanjay nodded thoughtfully. "She's right, you know, Stephen."

"Course I am," she grinned. "C'mon, let's

start work straight away. Jump to it, little brother!"

"Roll up, everybody, roll up," cried Jason at the next games lesson. "Come to the circus and see Stilts, the amazing skyscraper boy."

They all laughed once more at Stephen's long skinny legs and then, as usual, left him until last when they picked teams. None of them wanted to be lumbered with him.

"I'd rather be one man short than have the Eiffel Tower on our side," somebody joked.

"More like the Leaning Tower of Pisa, you mean," Jason cut in. "He always looks like he's just about to collapse!"

"Don't want to be on *your* side, anyway, " Stephen answered back. "You always lose."

"Rubbish!" Jason scoffed. "What does a stick insect know about football?"

"Ignore him," said Sanjay. "Come and join us instead, but don't try any headers today. We're not ready yet."

"I don't think I'll ever be ready. Emily almost gave up on me last night, I was so bad."

"Don't worry. Practice makes perfect, so they say."

"It makes me tired, I know that," Stephen sighed.

The game did not go well for him. Every time he made a mistake or mis-kicked the ball, he was jeered by his own side and cheered by the other. And when the teacher wasn't looking, he was tripped and pushed around by both.

The one moment Stephen did enjoy, though, was when Sanjay slipped the ball cheekily between Jason's legs and ran on to score a brilliant solo goal. The captain was furious. He

always boasted about his strong tackling and nobody had ever dared to trick him like that before.

"You wait, Patel. I'm going to dump you over the fence next time for that."

Sanjay grinned. "You'll have to catch me first."

He did. Later in the game, Jason hit him with a fierce, dangerous tackle, making no attempt to play the ball. He simply charged straight into Sanjay as the winger dribbled the ball towards goal and kicked him hard above the knee.

The teacher told Jason off for the foul but Sanjay saw that the boy was still smirking. He limped painfully away, even more determined now that, somehow, he would have his revenge one day.

And he knew which day he wanted it to be, too.

"Right, that does it," Sanjay said as Stephen came over to examine the stud marks on his skin. "It's about time that kid was shown up in front of all those mates of his. You and me are going to make him eat his words."

"Me? How can I help?" Stephen asked.

"By using your head," Sanjay replied with a wink. "How do you fancy coming to play for my Sunday League team? I reckon we could just do with somebody your size."

"But I'm no good. They won't want me. Nobody does."

"*I* do," Sanjay said firmly. "And I'm captain. We train together twice a week and you'll need all the extra practice you can get."

"Why, what's the rush?"

"Because we've got a big cup match soon against a team from a higher division that I really want to beat. Jason's team!"

"That's good, Stephen, well done. You're improving."

"I should think so, too," he gasped. "The way you've had me jumping up and down like a jack-in-the-box every night for weeks."

Emily let him rest at last. Her brother had worked hard, she had to admit, and she felt quite pleased with his progress.

"Well, you might never become footballer of the year," she smiled, pouring him a drink of orange. "But you could win a medal one day in the high jump!"

"Oh, thanks! At least I can jump *and* head a ball now, that's the main thing. Sanjay even reckons I'm better in the air than anybody he's seen."

Stephen grinned sheepishly at repeating his friend's compliment of the other evening. He didn't really believe it was true, of course, but it was still nice to hear. "Mind you," he added ruefully, "he probably only said that to make himself seem like the world's greatest coach."

It had all taken endless hours of practice and patience. Sanjay had first shown him how to head a ball properly with the forehead so that it wouldn't hurt. Then, as Stephen's confidence increased, so gradually did his power and accuracy.

Starting in the garden by aiming at a white square chalked on the side of the garage wall, Stephen had moved on to the real thing on the pitch in the Sunday team's training sessions. Sanjay hit crosses to him from the wing so that he could head towards an empty goal, praising Stephen every time he made firm contact and found the net.

"Great stuff!" he shouted after one spectacular diving effort. "No goalie would have smelt that.

Just wait till Jason's lot see you in action now. They'll get the shock of their lives."

Even Stephen himself was amazed. He actually enjoyed heading a ball so much, it no longer seemed to matter that his big clumsy feet still couldn't trap or kick it very well.

Not only that – and perhaps most amazing of all to Stephen – there was the fact of how friendly his new team-mates had turned out to be. Many of them were Asian like Sanjay and attended other schools, so had never come across him before, but he need not have worried how they would take to him.

The captain helped to break the ice immediately by introducing him with a joke. "Please, team, not too much leg-pulling, or you'll make him even lankier than he is already!"

His huge leaps and heading ability soon had them looking up to him in more ways than one, and Stephen found he didn't mind their gentle teasing when things went wrong, knowing it wasn't meant nastily as it was at school. He would simply grin and get on with the game, waiting to give as good as he got when somebody else made a mistake.

And there was no doubting everyone's delight when Stephen was finally chosen to play in the cup match.

As Sanjay announced all the names, he held up an extra long number 9 shirt, unable to resist a further little bit of teasing for the good of team spirit. "Making his debut, we have Stephen Jackson, our centre-forward on stilts!"

Stephen giggled along with the rest, but when news of his selection reached Jason's ears next day, the opposing soccer captain burst into fits of cruel laughter. "This has got to be some kind of joke."

"No joke," Sanjay informed him. "Stephen's our new striker."

"Striker! A grandfather clock can strike better than old Stilts! You must really be desperate if you've had to pick him."

"Only sorry you've found out now," Sanjay replied. "We wanted it to be a surprise."

"Oh, it'll still be a surprise all right," Jason hooted. "If you tell Stilts I'll be marking him it'll be a surprise if he even dares to turn up."

When Sanjay's team, including Stephen, *did* arrive for the game on the Sunday morning, Jason greeted them with yet more insults.

"You lot will be such push-overs, it was hardly worth getting out of bed for today," he jeered. "We could all have had a lie-in instead."

As expected, though, Stephen was Jason's main target. "You look like a great long stick of rock in those red and white stripes, Stilts. I think I might well take a few big bites out of you just to check."

Stephen glared at him. "Maybe you will, but we'll see who gets licked in the end," he answered back.

His retort made Jason angry. "Right, you're for it now, freak. We'll see how funny you find it after I've kicked you black and blue as well."

"The referee won't let you get away with fouling me all the time," Stephen replied bravely.

"Don't count on it," Jason snarled. "The ref's my uncle!"

"Goal!" Jason cried as his team went ahead in their very first attack. "You haven't even touched it yet, Stilts, and you're losing."

"Well you can't blame me for once then, can you?"

Jason flicked Stephen's ear spitefully. "Don't

be cheeky. At least you'll have a chance to kick-off every time we score. Think you can manage that without messing it up?"

Stephen kept quiet and rubbed his ear. He wasn't bothered about the number of kicks he got, not even those from Jason. It was the headers that mattered.

It soon became clear that the referee would indeed turn a blind eye to any dirty tactics. When Stephen received his first pass, Jason banged into him from behind to send him toppling to the ground, but play was waved on.

"*Foul*, ref!" came a scream from the touchline. It was Emily. She had travelled with the team to support her brother, and quickly realised he was going to need all the extra help he could get.

Out on the pitch at that moment, Stephen was actually receiving some more from Sanjay, who pulled him back up onto his feet.

"You need a crane for that job," Jason gloated, before switching his attack. "Hey, Stilts, is that your sister over there? She looks like a giant matchstick with that stupid red bobble hat on her head."

"Belt up, will you!" Sanjay cut in. "Go and pick on somebody your own size."

Jason would have lost his temper, if he hadn't suddenly seen the funny side of what Sanjay had just said. Even Stephen had to smile.

Despite their bad start, the visitors somehow remained only one goal down at half-time. That was mostly thanks to a great deal of luck and rebounds from the woodwork, but also to some outstanding saves from their overworked goalkeeper.

And they might even have scored themselves once when a rare attack resulted in a goalmouth scramble: the ball trickled out to Stephen, who only had to poke it over the line to equalise. Instead, he went and stubbed his toe on the ground, stumbled and ended up tapping the ball gently into the grateful keeper's hands.

Jason's team were helpless with laughter. Most of them played for the school, too, and Stephen turned bright red as they mocked him.

"Don't worry about it," Sanjay told him during the interval. "We've been practising with your head, not your feet."

But when at last, early in the second half, Sanjay did curl a high cross into the penalty area especially for him, Stephen missed it completely.

"I was pushed as I jumped," he complained bitterly to the referee.

The man smiled. "Sorry, lad, never saw anything."

Jason slipped his uncle a wink, but five minutes later the smirks were wiped off both their faces.

It was Sanjay again who broke free down the touchline and set up the chance. Jinking through two tackles, he looked up to see

Stephen making for the far post as they had practised so many times. The winger chipped the ball towards goal and watched Stephen and Jason go for it together.

Jason took off first, confident that he would head it clear easily, but then felt somebody soar past him. Next moment, the ball was bulging the top corner of the net. Captain and goalkeeper stared at one another in horror as Stephen ran off, punching the air in excitement, until he was caught and mobbed by his equally delighted team-mates.

"Just lucky," Jason yelled to cover his embarrassment. Nobody had outjumped him like that all season, but not even his uncle could find any reason to disallow the goal.

Nor the second one soon afterwards.

Sanjay swung a high corner right over everybody's heads in the crowded goalmouth. It looked as if it was going harmlessly away out of danger until Stephen suddenly charged into view from where he'd been lurking outside the penalty area.

He leapt up and seemed to hang in mid-air for a few moments before his head snapped forward like the spring on a mousetrap and the

ball rocketed into the net past the keeper's despairing dive.

"The winner!" squealed Emily, and she almost ran onto the pitch herself to hug her younger brother.

Her forecast proved correct. Stephen's two stunningly headed goals had knocked the stuffing out of Jason's team. Not used to losing, they were unable to fight back and slumped to a shock 2–1 defeat.

Jason could hardly believe it. He wanted to rush off home in shame, but first his players made him confront Stephen in the changing hut.

"Go on, ask him now," said one of them. "So we can all hear you."

"OK, OK, I'm going to, you don't have to push," Jason said, shrugging them off. "Er... just a minute, Stilts, before you go... "

"What do you want?"

The captain hesitated and swallowed hard. "Er... looks like we have to take back all the things we've said, after what you did to us today."

Sanjay came over quickly, grinning, and slapped Stephen on the back in congratulations.

"Magic headers, those, weren't they? Glad you liked them!"

Jason forced a sickly smile. "Yeah, well, because of them, right, we were wondering if he'd like to play centre-forward for the school team too from now on. What do you say, Stilts – er… I mean, Stephen?"

"That'd be great, I'd love to," he agreed straight away. "As long as there's no more stupid remarks about you-know-what."

"Not any more," Jason promised. "Seems I'll have to do some fast growing myself, if I'm going to be able to beat you in the air."

Stephen had never felt happier in his life. "I don't mind if you do sometimes call me Stilts, though," he said.

Jason blinked. "Why not? I thought you hated it."

"Guess I've kind of got used to it," Stephen smiled. "And anyway, it'll help to remind me of something very important."

"What's that?" asked Sanjay, caught by surprise too."

"Well, thanks to you and Emily, I've learnt how to make the most of my extra height," Stephen replied, suddenly serious. "I won't have to go around stooping any more, trying to hide it. I can walk tall at last now, just like those performers in the circus act!"

Gemma **t**he **G**ymnast

"Good pass, Gemma," the sports teacher called out across the court.

The Goal Defence gave no sign of having heard and Mrs Simpson ran over to her, wanting the girl to gain encouragement from the praise.

"Well played!" she said loudly, standing right in front of her.

Gemma grinned, pleased herself with the way she had caught and passed the ball. She knew she wasn't really good enough to be picked for Lynfield Primary School's netball team, but Gemma always looked forward to the lunchtime practice sessions. If nothing else, they helped to keep her fit for her favourite sport of gymnastics.

Today, however, her mind was more on the gym club after school. The names of those taking part in the county tournament were going to be announced and she was desperately hoping that hers would be among them.

"Watch out!" Her friend's warning shout had

no effect. By the time Karen's frantic arm-waving caught Gemma's attention, the opposing Goal Attack – free of her day-dreaming marker – had received the ball in a space and quickly moved it on to the Shooter.

The attacker ran into the goal circle to catch the return pass, unchallenged, and had enough time to take aim before Gemma could get back to try and block the shot. The ball looped up, wobbled on the ring and finally dropped through the net for a goal.

Louise, the scorer, gave Gemma a sly smirk. "Lost me again! You've no idea what's going on half the time, have you?"

The defender looked blankly at Louise's gloating face and sighed, glad at least not to hear any complaints from her own team-mates. They all knew it would just be a waste of breath.

The instant Mrs Simpson blew the whistle for the restart, Louise sped away, quick off the mark, nipping into the centre third to snap up the pass. Gemma hadn't reacted until her opponent darted forwards but now lunged across in an effort to intercept the ball from Louise herself. No luck! It was thrown well out of her reach and her team were in trouble again.

A further flurry of passes gave the Shooter a good scoring chance but despite lining the shot up carefully, she missed. As the ball rebounded from the ring, Gemma and Louise leapt high for it together and this time it was the defender

who triumphed.

Gemma timed her spring a fraction better to claim possession and then looked up to see Karen indicating she wanted the ball to her left. The Goal Defence obliged, sidestepped Louise to link up with the Centre once more, and the danger was cleared as the ball was hurled ahead to start another counter-attack.

That brief passage of play served to highlight Gemma's strengths – her agility to outjump opponents and dodge nimbly into spaces – and her main weakness. The thing that often let her down during a game was that she could all too easily be caught out of position.

It wasn't her fault. Unlike everyone else on the court, Gemma had to rely only on what she actually saw other players doing before she could respond. Little giveaway sounds of movement around her and people's calls went undetected – and so, too, did the umpire's whistle.

For Gemma was deaf: without wearing her special radio hearing aids, she could hardly hear a thing. Back in the changing room, Gemma fastened on all the equipment again but was still unable to follow the other girls' conversation properly. It was mostly just background babble until Karen tapped her on the shoulder and spoke directly to her.

"Do you want to come round to my house after gym club?" she asked.

"Sorry?" Gemma replied, handing her the transmitter.

Karen repeated her question and added, "You could stay for tea while we sort out some more ideas for each other's floor sequences."

"Don't even know yet if I'll be chosen for the tournament."

"You deserve to be, after all the extra practice you've been putting in recently."

"I need it," Gemma laughed, her voice becoming louder and jerkier with excitement. "My balances were all wobbly last week."

Karen was used to the odd way that Gemma spoke, but Louise nearby let out a snort. "What's she gabbling on about now? I don't know how you follow it all."

Karen turned on her sharply. "Because I listen, that's how, which is more than *you* ever do. You're always making fun of her voice."

"So what?" Louise challenged her. "Just sounds like a load of gibberish to me."

"That's a rotten thing to say," Karen cried. "How would you like it if *you* couldn't speak clearly because you were deaf?"

"Pardon?" Louise replied, cupping a hand to her ear in pretence, knowing it would enrage

Karen.

"Think you're so clever, don't you? Netball captain, county tennis player and everything. But you don't care a toss for other people's feelings. Well, Gemma's worth two of you."

"She certainly gets twice as much time as me from all the teachers. Don't see why she should cause so much extra bother in a place like this – she ought to be sent to a special school."

Karen knew she shouldn't keep rising to the bait, but she couldn't help it. Louise was the only one in the class who taunted Gemma, and Karen thought it was so unfair, especially as the victim did not always know what was being said about her. Everyone accepted her deafness and tolerated the need for the teacher to repeat things for Gemma's benefit at times and give her more individual attention.

"Wish *you* could be sent away," Karen said. "Somewhere completely on your own – then you might even be able to be top of the class."

"Ha, ha, very funny," Louise sneered. "I know why you'd like to get rid of me – 'cos I'm also the best gymnast in this school, not you. You're just jealous."

"Rubbish!" Karen snapped, angry with herself

at allowing Louise the chance for more stupid boasting. She tugged Gemma along towards the door, knowing her friend would have heard little of their argument. "C'mon, let's go. I want to get away from that bad smell."

"Bad smell?" Gemma echoed. "I can't smell anything."

"It's sitting over there on the bench," Karen replied, looking pointedly at the player still wearing the red GA bib from the practice.

Louise sniggered, trying to turn Karen's parting jibe back against Gemma in order to save face in front of the other netballers. "Oh dear, our poor little deaf girl's losing her sense of smell as well, now!"

A few of them giggled, more to keep in favour with Louise than in amusement at her less than funny remark. But at least Elizabeth, the captain's best friend, felt able to speak her mind.

"Wish you'd leave off her, Louise. Gemma's OK when you really get to know her. She never uses her deafness as an excuse if she makes a mistake at anything."

"*When* she makes mistakes, you mean. What about the game? She was hopeless."

"Come off it, she didn't play that badly. Anybody finds it hard trying to mark you."

Elizabeth's flattery helped to put Louise in a better mood again. "OK, OK, so she can't help being deaf, I know that. I'll say sorry to her later on – as long as she's not got her gear tuned in to Radio One!"

"Don't talk daft," said Elizabeth. "But you ought to make friends – we might all be in the same team for the gym tournament."

"What!" Louise was genuinely astonished, not having given Gemma's chances of selection much thought. "Anyway, won't make any difference to me if she is picked. Her big buddy, Karen, will just have to look after her. Mrs Simpson knows I've got better things to do."

"And what's that?"

"Getting top marks – I'm going to be the new county gym champion."

"Careful, Karen hold that balance for longer," Mrs Simpson urged her as she supervised the gym club in the school hall. "Point those toes more, Elizabeth. Come on, stretch out, now."

The gymnasts were warming up for the more demanding work to come later, enabling the coach to wander among them making observations. Mrs Simpson stood for a while watching Gemma going through a series of flexibility exercises, trying so hard to impress as always. On form, she could be an excellent gymnast, but…

Doubts continued to nag at the coach's mind about including Gemma in the team. She tried to convince herself that Gemma's balances on the beam weren't always reliable, and that her vaulting sometimes lacked the desired spring and power. But, if she were to be honest with herself, she had to admit the main stumbling block was the deafness problem.

The girl wasn't able to wear her hearing aids when doing sport, making communication difficult. "Gemma," Mrs Simpson began, but there was no response at first until the coach signalled to her. "Show me your bridge, please. Bridge!"

Gemma nodded and lay down on her back, knees bent. Upside-down, there was no way she could even attempt to use her basic lip-reading skills to receive any instructions but, in this case, no further help was needed. She pushed herself up into a bridge shape easily, straightening her

arms and legs to achieve a graceful, high arch.

"Good, lovely," the coach said after the gymnast flipped herself back up onto her feet. She also gave her the thumbs-up sign for extra effect to ensure the message of praise was understood.

"*Lovely!*" Louise mimicked under her breath on a nearby mat. "Huh! Any half-decent five-year-old could have done that just as well."

She tried to catch Elizabeth's eye so she could pull a face in mockery but her friend was too busy doing some backward rolls. Louise decided to show off instead to anyone who might be watching. She kicked herself up into a perfectly controlled handstand, holding it for several seconds before letting her body overbalance smoothly into a forward roll, to finish in a wide straddle position.

It was a tough session. Mrs Simpson worked them hard, concentrating on vaulting and insisting on a strong, fast run-up and good flight, both onto and off the vaulting horse. She positioned the springboard well away from the apparatus and landings also had to be spot-on in order to receive her nod of approval. According to their level of ability, the gymnasts practised a variety of vaults, some straddles and squats, some handsprings and necksprings, expertly supported by the coach at the side with steadying, guiding hands.

There was also time, however, for further work on the mats and low beam to improve their rolls and balances while Mrs Simpson finally made up her mind which six girls to take to the tournament. Louise, Karen and Elizabeth were obvious choices, but many other keen and talented young gymnasts would have to be disappointed. Gemma, reluctantly, was going to be one of them.

Gathering the group together right at the end, Mrs Simpson broke the good and bad news, announcing also that the tournament was to be held at the main sports centre in the county.

"Hey, great!" Louise enthused. "That's where I go training with the county squad. It's a massive place – and they're even building another extension to it."

Gemma struggled to hold back the tears afterwards in the changing room. " I didn't miss my name, did I? It wasn't mentioned?"

"No, sorry, but it should have been," Karen said, trying to console her. "You were vaulting really well."

"Thanks. I'll still come along, though, to cheer you on."

"Hoped you would. It'll help me to put up with that big-head, Louise," Karen said with a grimace. "Fancy her being made captain of this, too. She won't be interested in how the team is getting on at all. The only thing she's after is the individual award."

"Perhaps you might even pip Louise yourself with a bit of luck."

"With a lot of luck, you mean. She is good, I have to admit. It's just that she knows it – and makes sure everybody else knows it too!"

"Not me."

"How do you avoid having to suffer all her bragging, then?"

"Easy." Gemma managed a chuckle. "I just flick the switch on my receiver here and turn her off!"

"Reckon we could all do with one of those at times," Karen said, only half in jest. "A mute-Louise button!"

How Gemma would have loved to join in

with the team's extra training sessions! She was always there, supporting their efforts and watching enviously as Karen worked with Deepa, a Hindu girl, on their pairs routine – a mixture of synchronised moves and balances together.

But when the chance to do so came out of the blue, Gemma almost wished that it hadn't. Misfortune struck Lynfield's preparations only a week before the tournament with Elizabeth, one of the school's best gymnasts, injuring herself while vaulting.

She landed awkwardly from a straddle jump, crumpling up with a yelp of pain and grasping her ankle with both hands. As everyone anxiously gathered round, Mrs Simpson lifted her onto a chair at the side of the hall to inspect the damage. Whenever she pressed gently around the area, Elizabeth winced and stifled another cry.

"Sorry, my love, no more gym for a while, I'm afraid," Mrs Simpson told her sympathetically. "There's nothing broken, I'm sure, but you've badly twisted your ankle."

"But what about the tournament?" Elizabeth asked, tears brimming up into her eyes at the thought of missing it. The look on the coach's face confirmed her worst fears and she hugged herself in silent misery.

Gemma was the one who helped Elizabeth to dress as the others finished off. "I'm ever so sorry for you, Lizzie," she said.

"You don't really mean that, of course," said Elizabeth bitterly – and then wished she hadn't when she saw the hurt on Gemma's face. "Oh, I'm sorry, too. You haven't even thought about it yet, have you?"

Gemma still looked blank and Elizabeth sighed. "My bad luck is your good luck. While I'm sitting in the doctor's, Mrs Simpson will be asking you to take my place in the team."

The forecast proved correct. Gemma's concern for Elizabeth, and the way she had been helping the other gymnasts train, persuaded the coach that, with time now so short, Gemma was the one who most deserved to fill the gap.

As Gemma left for home all excited with Karen, Mrs Simpson also informed her captain of the team change. Louise had been quite upset at losing her best friend, but now she felt even more sorry for herself. The thought of Gemma as her new pairs partner hit her like a wet sponge.

"Can't it be someone else?" she asked in desperation. "I mean, well, won't being like she is cause problems?"

"Possibly," the teacher conceded, "but nothing we can't solve, I'm sure, by working together. You and Gemma will need to see a lot of each other over the next week."

Louise groaned to herself under her breath. "Huh! We might *see* each other, but that's about all. She can't hear and I won't listen… "

Gemma was soon to surprise them both. She invited Karen to stay for tea, and the two of them put the finishing touches to plans for Gemma's floorwork routine. It had already been drawn in a series of diagrams some weeks before and now they discussed possible linking moves to help the sequence of rolls, springs and balances flow together more smoothly.

Gemma had listened to the brief piece of taped music so many times that she knew it off by heart, hearing it being replayed inside her head more clearly than Karen did on the cassette player. Putting their previous ballet class training to good use, they practised little

dance movements that Gemma could perform for artistic effect and spent two enjoyable hours clumping around the bedroom.

"We'll show Mrs Simpson she should have picked you in the first place," Karen grinned. "She won't believe her eyes when she sees you in action tomorrow doing all this stuff."

The coach was indeed amazed. She watched it through twice and although the backflips and handsprings needed some improvement, Gemma covered the whole matted area well and confidently. What made her performance all the more impressive was that during the second go, Mrs Simpson turned the tape off and the gymnast didn't even know!

Louise, too, was caught off guard. She had been dreading having to try and explain all the activities that she and Elizabeth had been putting together but, in fact, Gemma remembered most of it from watching them at work. Her new partner picked things up quicker than Louise had expected, and they developed a little secret sign language of nods and winks when it was Gemma's turn to do something. By the end of their third session, Gemma was suggesting changes and adding extra touches of her own, proving herself stronger than Elizabeth and able to support Louise in balancing acts more steadily. As their trust in each other grew, they began to explore moves and positions that would otherwise have been impossible.

Louise also discovered Gemma's sense of humour, laughing aloud over some of the things she came out with as they worked together. She found she was not laughing *at* the deaf girl as she used to, but laughing *with* her instead.

Gemma had seen a different side to Louise, too. "She was a bit bossy at first, but we're getting on fine now," Karen heard her friend remark on the way home one day. "She's all right, really, when you get to know her better."

Karen smiled. "That's exactly what we've been telling her about you for ages! Now she's found out for herself, she'll probably go round claiming the credit for it."

They giggled and then Gemma became suddenly serious. "Just hope I don't go and spoil things, that's all. I'd hate to let her and you and everybody else in the team down."

"'Course you won't," Karen reassured her. "Everything will be just perfect on Saturday, you'll see."

"What's all that banging?"
"What a racket!"
"Hope it's not going to carry on during the

competition."

More and more voices were raised in complaint as teams of gymnasts arrived at the sports centre for the county tournament. The hall echoed to the sound of hammering and drilling from the construction work that was taking place outside.

"We must apologise for the distracting level of noise," came the official announcement over the tannoy in between more bangs. "The work on the extension to the building is behind schedule and cannot stop for the gymnastics. Please try to ignore it as best you can, everybody."

"Ignore it, the man says," Louise sneered. "It's deafening! We're all going to end up like Gemma at this rate."

Her remark was not aimed spitefully at her team-mate as might once have been the case, but this time almost in envy. She could see her dream of becoming county champion turning into a nightmare.

"Is it really bad?" Gemma asked. "It all sounds a bit muffled to me."

"You're lucky," Karen replied. "Don't know how we're going to put up with it right through the afternoon."

"Well, I'm going to get rid of it," said Gemma and started to remove her hearing aid equipment, storing all the bits and pieces in her sports bag for safe keeping. "There, that's better, nice and quiet now."

"What did you say?" asked Karen.

"Sorry?"

"Say it again," Karen told her, speaking face to face. " I couldn't hear you because of the noise."

"Er... I said it's all gone quiet," Gemma repeated, sheepishly.

"Might have for you," Louise butted in grumpily. "What about *me*? How do they expect me to concentrate?"

"Same for all of us, I guess," Karen murmured.

"Not quite," Louise corrected her, nodding towards Gemma, who was now gazing wide-eyed at the large numbers of spectators, mostly parents and families of the gymnasts. She understood that groups of girls would be doing different events in separate areas of the sports hall, but had never expected the place to be so big – and so busy.

When the competition began, it soon became

clear that the children were not indeed all affected in the same way by outside interference.

While some competitors were fortunate enough to perform a particular exercise during an occasional lull, others were accompanied by constant grating sounds. Worse still, if they were especially unlucky, their concentration was ruined by a sudden loud crash, causing them to topple from the beam or be put off in the middle of their floor sequence.

Deepa was one to suffer like that but she was at least able to see the funny side to it. "That last big crash made me jump so much, I never even needed the springboard to do my vault!" she joked to the others in the Lynfield base afterwards.

"It's when it does go quiet for a bit that it worries me," Karen put in. "All the time I was working on the beam, I was just waiting for another bang. The suspense was killing!"

"How did you get on?" Deepa asked.

"OK, I think, amazingly, but I haven't heard my score yet. Even the judges are struggling to add up, I reckon, with all the noise going on!"

At this point Louise stormed back into the base, nearly in tears with anger and frustration. Normally the safest and most graceful of movers along the beam, she had been jerked off-balance by an unexpected screech of machinery and only saved herself from falling off the apparatus by some wild arm-waggling and sheer determination to stay on.

"This whole thing's a farce," she moaned

bitterly. "Months of hard work all wasted. It's just not fair."

Mrs Simpson was sympathetic. "I've suggested to the organisers that the tournament should be cancelled in case somebody gets hurt," she said, glancing at Elizabeth who had come along to watch with her ankle still strapped up. "But they insist it will carry on."

Much of the audience's sympathy went out to the girls trying to complete their floorwork to a background of noise. Their efforts were applauded generously, even more so if they had failed to keep in time and rhythm with music that they could hardly hear.

Louise, when her turn came round on the mats, was one of the lucky ones. She benefited from a quiet period and performed her well-rehearsed routine beautifully, but Karen saw her chances of winning a medal disappear in what was usually her best exercise.

"It was that terrible drilling sound," Karen explained sadly. "I've gone through my sequence dozens of times back at school but it just got drummed out of my head today. I was making the moves up as I went along in the end."

"You managed very well in the circumstances," the coach praised her. "The judges will have known you went wrong, of course, but most people probably won't even have noticed."

"Good luck, Gemma," Karen said, content now to try and assist her friend as planned. "I'll give you a wave, remember, to let you know when your music starts."

Gemma watched Karen's lips and picked up the gist of what she was saying, helped by a little mime of waving. "And give me a kick as well when my name is called out," she said with a grin.

"Don't worry, it won't happen again," Karen promised, knowing how close Gemma had already come to being disqualified for missing her cue. If it hadn't been for Louise, she would now be out of the competition.

Gemma had been left by herself in the base briefly while everyone was busy elsewhere, when Louise suddenly appeared and slapped her on the back of her bright blue leotard. "C'mon, hasn't anybody told you? Your name's been called twice for the beam."

Seeing Gemma hadn't understood, Louise grabbed her by the arm and hauled her off to the judges' table near the apparatus. They arrived only just in time.

"Where have you been, girl?" said one of the judges crossly when she reported in at last. "Are you deaf or something?"

Gemma stared at him, aware he was speaking to her and that he didn't seem pleased. He took her lack of response as insolence until Louise spoke up. "Er... yes, she is deaf, actually, so she didn't hear her name announced at all."

The man reddened in embarrassment. "Oh, right, sorry, young lady. Please forgive me. All this noise making me a bit short-tempered, I'm afraid."

"Apology's no use, mister, she can't hear that either," Louise said cheekily and saw her chance to make her own feelings known. "It's a pity we weren't all given free ear-plugs this afternoon!"

He waved Louise away in irritation and signalled Gemma towards the apparatus. She felt good standing there in front of the crowd, full of confidence after two fine vaults and knowing that most other girls had been making mistakes. If she could just keep her nerve on the ten-centimetre-wide beam of padded wood ...

This wasn't her favourite exercise, but she

mounted cleanly and began her routine of balances, rolls, steps, leaps and turns with barely a wobble. Suddenly there came the loudest crash of the day, as if something had been dropped from the top of the scaffolding. It made everyone inside the centre start – everyone except the gymnast on the beam who carried on without even flinching.

Gemma's mind was fixed firmly on her movements, stretching to achieve good body tension and remembering to keep her head up and show that she was enjoying it. She was! She finished with a handstand dismount, landing nicely on her toes and then standing to attention for the judges and a huge round of applause from the audience. Gemma saw the people clapping madly and thought it must be for something going on elsewhere.

After her star turn on the beam, the spectators were watching for Gemma's mop of fair hair to appear on the mats.

They had no idea of her handicap, didn't see her waved into action from the side as the music began and never realised she couldn't hear it. The fact that it was almost drowned out by the din from outside anyway made her dashing display seem all the more remarkable.

Gemma rounded her floorwork off with a back somersault, followed by a graceful, balletic sweep of the arms to interpret the last few notes – a little extra flourish she'd decided to slip in at the end that not even Karen nor Mrs Simpson had seen before – and then ran excitedly back to the home base to receive her friends' congratulations.

Louise joined in the praise, already resigned to the belief that she herself was unlikely now to win the individual county title. But with Gemma in such peak form, she had set her sights instead on the pairs championship.

"Well done," she said to her partner, wrapping an arm round her shoulders and mouthing her words clearly. "But calm down, it's not all over yet. We've still got some more work to do."

They were one of the first pairs to perform their act and the watching Elizabeth was quite happy to admit that she could scarcely have supported and linked up with Louise better. What the week-old partnership lacked slightly in fluent co-ordination was more than made up for by the inventiveness of their balances together and the high quality of gymnastic ability shown by both of the girls. They set a standard that no other pair could match and were rightly judged as winners, although Karen and Deepa snatched second place with a lively, imaginative joint routine of their own.

To Mrs Simpson's great surprise and delight, the tournament proved an overwhelming success for Lynfield School. On top of the double triumph in the pairs, Louise came first in the floorwork exercise, Gemma won the beam and was also third on the mats, and all six girls' efforts were rewarded with runners-up spot in the team competition.

To crown everything else, however, Gemma was awarded the main honour when her overall points total made her the new primary school age county gymnastics champion!

Gemma even heard her own name announced this time. While the marks were being sorted out, she had refitted her hearing aids and marched proudly out to receive her trophy and certificates wearing all her bulky equipment with its leads trailing down over her leotard. The loud and long applause from the astonished audience was sweet music to her ears.

Louise was standing nearby, given third place individually, and Gemma leaned across to thank her again for saving her from possible disqualification. "I'd never have won this today but for you."

The captain managed a rueful smile at missing out on the real glory herself. "Yeah, well, it was sort of my duty wasn't it? Mind you, I didn't think then that you'd go on to become champion."

"Sorry?"

Louise grinned. "I was just wondering how you did it, champ!"

"Guess I was the only one who could turn a deaf ear to all the noise," Gemma chuckled. "Two deaf ears, in fact!"

Flash Back

"What's *she* doing back here?"

"Who?"

"Look out the window."

"I don't believe it! Reckoned we'd seen the last of her."

"Never thought she'd dare show her face round here again."

"Well she has – and I'd like to know why," demanded Kevin, the first of the boys to have spotted her.

They jostled for position near the windows, trying to get a better look, and then almost staggered back together, stunned by what they saw. Unaware of their attention, Natalie had pulled off her coat as she led a bunch of footballers across the playground towards the cloakroom area. For the gawping audience, the sight of her own all-white soccer kit was made even more shocking by its stark contrast against her black skin.

Natalie sucked in a deep breath, bracing herself for the coming ordeal. How she wished

she could be anywhere else right now but back at this hated school, a place of so many unhappy memories.

"This way, team," the home players heard her call out. "You can finish getting changed in here."

Natalie was the first figure in the doorway and she stopped short, confronted by a wall of familiar, hostile faces. She remembered the last time she had seen them, in this very room, only too well...

"Right, you're for it now, thief."

"Yeah, caught in the act at last, sneaking in here to nick stuff."

Natalie, startled, found herself surrounded by four or five boys who had suddenly leapt out from behind a rack of coats. They began pushing and pulling her from one to another across their tight, sneering circle.

"Thought this cloakroom was empty, didn't you?"

"Well, we were guardin' it, see, to nab you."

"Leave me alone," she pleaded. "I haven't done anything wrong."

The group of lads laughed cruelly into her face.

"Listen to Little Miss Innocence!" cackled Kevin. "Tell her what we're gonna do to her, Ben."

His mate leered. "We're goin' to teach you a lesson, Black Nat, that's what. Teach you not to go nickin' all our things."

"I'm not the thief!" she screamed, wide-eyed in fear. "It's… "

"Liar!" Kevin yelled before she could finish. "Everybody knows it's you. We're gonna get you chucked out of this school. Get you sent back to that kids' home in the city where you belong."

Natalie's violent response took Kevin by complete surprise. Before he could raise his hands, either in attack or defence, she had launched herself at him, scratching his cheeks with her nails. Then she was away, bursting through their clutches and out of the cloakroom door.

"Get after her, quick," Ben ordered. "She'll be easy to catch."

They tried. Madly giving chase, they tore outside, knocking over any small child who happened to wander into their path. Only on reaching the other side of the soccer pitch did they realise that the gap between them and Natalie was not in fact closing, as expected, but actually increasing.

Panting, they stopped and watched the fugitive disappear through the far gate of the large playing fields into the village streets.

"Had no idea she was that fast, did you?" gasped Jonathan, the school soccer captain.

Ben shook his head. "Incredible, the way she just took off like that."

"She's quick with her claws, too," Kevin growled, wiping away a smear of blood with his sleeve. "Look what she went and did to me. She's really had it now, I'll tell you – I'm gonna kill her next time!"

It was just as well for everyone, perhaps, that there had never been a next time. Until today.

Since that incident, over six months ago, orphan Natalie had not set foot back into Orchard Primary School. Her white foster parents, upset at their failure to protect the girl from all the name-calling and bullying she suffered, had sadly decided to return her to the care of the local authority.

Now, standing once more in front of her previous tormentors, Natalie felt the urge to flee again, prevented only by the excited surge of her team-mates pushing her through into the cloakroom.

"Well, well, fancy seeing you here this morning. What are you, the team's mascot?" Jonathan greeted her sarcastically.

Natalie didn't reply and the whole room fell silent for a few moments. There were no teachers present yet; they were still talking outside about the wet and windy conditions for the important County Cup game.

Ben, it was, who took advantage of their absence to make it clear to the visitors that she wasn't welcome. "Girls aren't allowed in here on match days, so get her out."

He'd been about to add some further comment as usual about her colour, until he realised that over half the team from Millbank School were black or Asian, too. He hesitated, and it gave Kevin the chance to make his presence felt, striding forward to fill the space between the two sets of players.

Natalie's heart sank. She'd been praying that Kevin might not even be playing, never mind being the opposing goalkeeper. Compared to the pale blue-striped shirts of the others, his bright yellow jersey with its dark zigzag markings made him look like an angry, buzzing bee.

He totally ignored Natalie, however, and issued a direct warning to those behind her instead. "Shouldn't leave money or nothing in your coats, if I were you. She's only brought you in here so she knows where your peg is."

"That's not fair," Natalie cried, turning to appeal to her new friends. "Don't listen to him. I told you what they were like. This one was always horrible to me."

"It's OK, Flash," Gurpreet said. "Won't matter what they say."

"Flash! Is that what you lot call her?" Kevin

67

snorted, and then he remembered her speed of movement. "Yeah, come to think of it, she was pretty quick at whipping other people's stuff."

"Shut it, man. Flash isn't here to be no mascot – she's our skipper today," Millbank's usual captain, Darryl, cut in, jabbing a finger at the goalkeeper. "Give her any hassle and you'll have to deal with all of us."

"Hear that, lads," Kevin scoffed. "The thief's got her own gang now. Better make sure Smithy locks away any valuables."

It was only the timely arrival onto the scene of the two sports teachers which probably prevented a fight from breaking out.

"Hello, what's going on here?" Mr Smith demanded, walking in first and immediately sensing the tension in the air. Then he noticed Natalie, partly shielded by team-mates who had stepped protectively in front of her. "Oh, my goodness, it's you! Didn't even know you were at Millbank now. Come back to watch the big match, have we?"

Natalie remained expressionless. She had no wish to appear friendly towards someone whom she felt had not really believed her denials about the stealing. She merely moved out into full view to reveal her soccer kit and her former teacher's mouth dropped open, lost for words.

Millbank's Mr Wilson tried to cover the other man's embarrassment. "Natalie soon showed she had quite a flair for the game when she joined in one of our practices," he explained. "She's so quick, too, a natural all-round athlete – as I'm sure you know."

Natalie continued to return Mr Smith's stare, knowing he had no idea about her sporting talents. She had never been given any encouragement at Orchard Primary to show what she could do on the playing field. Even in games lessons, she had been too nervous to perform well, afraid of what others might say.

It was all so different at Millbank in the middle of the city. For a start, they didn't even have any grass…

"Reckon you'll win the sprint on Sports Day easy," Gurpreet told the new girl after the summer term's first outdoor P.E. lesson.

Natalie smiled, pleased at receiving a rare compliment. "Didn't know this school had a sports field."

"We don't," he said. "Only got this hard playground. You just have to make sure you don't fall over, that's all!"

Gurpreet chuckled, recalling how she had outrun everybody. "The look on Darryl's face when you beat him in that final race. He couldn't believe it. He's always boasted he's the fastest boy in the school."

"He still is," she replied, and then winked. "He's just not the fastest pupil any more!"

Natalie suddenly looked worried. "Hope he won't take it out on me. I had enough of that kind of thing at my old place."

"No, Darryl's OK," he replied, before adding with a grin, "just so long as you're not better at football than him too!"

"You don't play football on here as well, do you?"

"Practices, yeah, but we have to play all our matches away."

"I've never played football," she admitted.

"Well, girls don't, do they?" Gurpreet said. "They can't kick a ball properly, or head it, or tackle and that like us boys do."

"Want a bet?" Natalie challenged him. "Let me join in the kickabout at lunchtime and we'll see. Go on, I dare you."

Gupreet sighed. "Oh, oh, after what you did to him this morning, I don't think Darryl's going to like this!"

To his surprise, however, Darryl liked what he saw very much. Already named by Mr Wilson as next season's soccer captain, he was taking the job seriously, always on the look-out for new talent.

"Man, just look at that, will you?" he said to Gurpreet as they took a break from the hectic game to watch Natalie perform. "The way she went past that kid – like a flash of lightning, she was."

"You reckon she's OK?"

"Sure, she's magic. With that pace, if she played on the wing, defenders would never catch her."

He called out to her. "Hey, Flash, come here, will you?"

Natalie didn't respond until he bellowed again. "Who are you shouting at? Me?"

"Who d'yer think?"

"But my name's Natalie."

"Not any more, it ain't," Darryl grinned. "We're all gonna call you Flash – I've decided!"

"Tails!" Natalie called out as Mr Smith tossed the spinning coin into the air and let it plop onto the squelchy centre-spot.

Jonathan smirked as they caught sight of the Queen's head lying in the mud. "We'll kick with the wind first half. Build up a big lead."

Natalie groaned to herself. That had been her plan as well – their only hope, she thought, of winning.

Her captaincy had not exactly got off to the best of starts. Besides the nastiness in the cloakroom, she'd also had to take a whole stack of insults on the way out to the pitch from several Orchard players, making it quite clear what they intended to do to Millbank – and to her, too, given half a chance.

Now, when she believed that things couldn't get any worse, they did. Much worse. Firstly, taking up her usual position out on the left-wing for the kick-off, she found herself sloshing through long wet grass, the kind of swampy conditions which made trying to run with the ball an impossible task. Secondly, she saw Ben waiting for her on the right-hand side of the Orchard defence.

"I'm the lucky one with the job of markin' you," he hooted, and then turned the taunt into a threat. "And I'll mark you all right, Black Nat – you're goin' to be scarred for life by the time this match is over."

He started as he meant to carry on. As Orchard went straight on to the attack and all eyes were watching the play at the other end, Ben barged heavily into her, catching her a spiteful crack on the back of the leg with his boot.

Natalie's shinpad gave her no protection there and she yelped in pain, much to his delight. "Just a taste of what's to come. They're the only kicks you're goin' to get this game – from me!"

Nobody had seen the foul and Natalie retreated deep into her own half to try and keep out of his way for a while. But as soon as the ball came to her, Ben pounced. He tackled her fiercely from behind before she had even managed to control it, upending her at the same time as smacking the ball out of play.

Mr Smith only gave a throw-in rather than a free kick, and Natalie sat in a puddle of water for a second, feeling very sorry for herself. She wished she'd never let them talk her into returning to play in this cup match at all. She'd been dreading it ever since the news of the draw...

"Sir's just told me who we've got in the next round," Darryl yelled, bursting into the classroom where most of the footballers were spending their playtime, sheltering from the heavy rain.

"Next round of what?" Gurpreet asked, without thinking.

"The County Cup, stupid!" Darryl grinned. "And guess what. Sir says we're up against one of Flash's old schools, Orchard Primary."

Natalie exclaimed aloud in dismay. "Oh, no, sorry, I can't go back there. You'll just have to do without me, I'm afraid."

"What d'yer mean?" Darryl gasped. "Course you'll be playing – in fact, we want you to be our captain that day. It's a kind of tradition, like, when somebody meets their old pals again."

"Pals!" Natalie snorted. "You've got to be joking. I never want to see any of them again in my life."

"C'mon, Flash," Gurpreet urged her. "We know they gave you a bad time, but you can't turn down a chance like this to be skipper."

Natalie hesitated, under pressure from the others, as well, to agree. "But if I'm playing, it'll only make everything much harder for us. They hated me. They wouldn't be able to bear the thought of losing."

"Rubbish!" cried Darryl, running his hand

through his closely-cropped black curls, as he often did when arguing. "Even better if you get them mad — they won't be able to play properly."

"From what you've said," put in Luke, the Millbank goalie, "it might have been better if you'd stayed and tried to prove them all wrong."

Natalie shook her head. "No, they were just so awful to me, Luke. I couldn't stand it any longer so I ran away."

"Is that why you can run so fast?" Gurpreet ribbed her and they all had a giggle together, making her feel a bit better.

"Glad you ended up here, Flash, anyway," said Darryl. "Don't know how we'd have got on this season without your speed in attack and those deadly left-foot crosses of yours."

That was praise indeed coming from Darryl, the team's top scorer. She felt she couldn't refuse to play after that, but wasn't able to tell them much about their cup opponents. "No idea what they're like, really. I wasn't interested in football then."

"You must remember something," Darryl persisted.

Natalie shrugged, then vaguely recalled Ben and Kevin showing off in class one day after assembly. "Hold on, I think they must have won their league or cup last year 'cos they all got medals."

"Medals!" Gurpreet breathed in envy. "Hey, they must be pretty good, then."

"Bound to be, man," Darryl scoffed. "Big posh village school like that. We're gonna have to be on top form to beat 'em, for Flash's sake – pay 'em back for all them things they done to her."

Orchard's first goal went in after only five minutes of the game, the result of a long kick downwind from Kevin which sailed over the heads of the Millbank defenders.

It was Jonathan who finally gained control of the awkwardly bouncing ball and lashed it with great delight into the top corner of the net.

"Hope your teacher's brought a calculator," Ben shouted at Natalie as they lined up again after the home team's celebrations. "He's goin' to need it to keep count of the score."

Natalie ignored him, and was soon more concerned with trying to help her hard-pressed defence prevent further goals as Orchard continued to attack almost non-stop. Whereas Kevin could afford to lean idly on his goalpost, Luke was the busiest – and muddiest – player on the field, throwing himself in all directions to keep out the flood of shots.

It was, therefore, totally against the run of play when Millbank suddenly broke out of their own half to snatch an undeserved equaliser.

The Orchard defenders, Ben included, had grown careless, more eager to join in with their own team's attacks than keep an eye out for any of their opponents. Gurpreet caught them all out of position with an accurate pass through to Darryl who ran from the halfway line, unchallenged, to tuck the ball coolly past the goalkeeper.

Kevin went berserk. "You wallies couldn't even mark a page of sums!" he screamed. "Just make sure Black Nat doesn't get a chance to shoot, that's all, or I'll hang the lot of you on my crossbar!"

Up to that point, in fact, Natalie had enjoyed very few touches of the ball. But just a minute before half-time, she got the final contact in a goalmouth scramble that gave her no pleasure at all.

She put through her own goal.

Following a short corner, Ben hammered the ball hard and low into the Millbank penalty area, where it ricocheted crazily around like a bullet in a cave. Twice Luke saved from point-blank range, once the ball was cleared off the

line, but finally, as another shot looked like zooming wide of the target, Natalie stretched out a leg and deflected it out of reach of her groping goalkeeper.

Her team-mates were horrified for their captain, but they were unable to save her from all the ridicule being heaped upon her head by many of the Orchard players. Ben even ran forward to ruffle her hair in mockery before narrowly avoiding Gurpreet's reckless kick at him.

"Not your fault, you couldn't help it," Mr Wilson told a tearful Natalie at half-time, trying in vain to comfort her.

"I knew it was a big mistake to come back here," she whimpered. "I just can't do anything right today."

"Don't talk daft!" said Darryl. "C'mon, team, we've got the wind behind us this half, remember. Plenty of time left to make that lot sorry they ever upset our Flash, eh?"

The mood in the other camp was bubbly, all the boys joking about the own goal and predicting how many more they were going to score. Even Mr Smith's attempts to warn them about the dangers of over-confidence were treated lightly.

"Just be careful," he advised. "Don't let them pinch another goal like you did before."

"Yeah!" Kevin called out. "You all know how good Black Nat is at pinching things!"

"Wonder if she's still got my pen," laughed one defender.

"And mine," echoed another.

"Took my dinner money, she did," complained someone else, as the list of supposed crimes swiftly built up.

"Reckon that own goal helps to make up for her nicking Mr Smith's wallet from his jacket that time," Kevin cackled, quite carried away.

When the other players suddenly went quiet, puzzled, Ben decided it was time to bend down and refasten his bootlace. It was news to them that the teacher had also been one of Natalie's victims. Mr Smith, too, looked at his goalkeeper intently.

"Kevin, nobody knew about my missing wallet," he said slowly. "I never made that public, as I wasn't even certain I'd lost it at school. The only other person who could have known was the one who stole it."

The boy looked around his friends desperately for support, wishing he could bite off his own tongue. "Well, I... well, guess she... she must have told me sometime. You know, bragged about it, like... "

"Kevin, I think you had better go home before I get very, very angry," Mr Smith told him. "I happen to know it can't have been Natalie who took my wallet. I checked. She wasn't even at school that day... "

The Orchard players were struck dumb. It was only later that some of them began to recall how quick Kevin had been to accuse Natalie every time something went missing... how he always seemed to know about thefts almost before the people concerned had realised themselves...

"What's goin' on over there?" Darryl asked in frustration as the Millbank team waited impatiently to get under way for the second half. "They're takin' ages. Anyone would think they've got problems, not us."

"Probably hoping if they delay long enough, the wind will die down," Gurpreet suggested, only half in jest.

It was at this moment that they saw the Orchard goalkeeper, clearly distressed, throw down his yellow jersey and go running off the field.

"Looks like he's been sent off!" Gurpreet gasped.

"That's Kevin," Natalie said, giving a little shrug. "Probably said something he shouldn't, as usual. Good riddance to him."

"Good news, anyway," Gurpreet added. "Gives us more of a chance."

"If we ever kick off," Darryl remarked dryly.

To Natalie's surprise, Ben began to pull on the goalie top. Her spirits soared, knowing that he wouldn't be breathing down her neck any longer. When a stern-faced Mr Smith finally blew the whistle, and she found herself marked instead by a rather nervous-looking substitute, she even managed a smile for the first time that morning.

"C'mon, men, let's try and make things tough for the new keeper," she cried, playing the part of a real captain at last. "I want to see how this bully boy likes it, being on the receiving end for a change… "

"Hey, what are you up to in here?"

At first Natalie thought she'd been spotted and instinctively sank down deeper into the tight space between the cloakroom wall and a large wooden cabinet. It was her secret hiding place whenever she needed to keep out of the way of the bullies.

She'd recognised Ben's harsh voice and feared the question had been aimed at her. It was only when Kevin answered, that she once again peeped out to see him desperately trying to cram the things he'd been stealing into the nearest bag. Unknown to him, she'd been watching his actions for several minutes.

"Er, hiya, Ben," he called out. "Wait there, just coming."

"They're not our racks," Ben persisted, going over to take a closer look. "What... ?"

He stopped dead in his tracks as Kevin spilled some sweets and coins onto the floor in his guilty haste, and the two friends looked at each other for a moment in mutual embarrassment.

As the culprit bent to scoop them up, Ben nodded slowly. "You're the one who's been nickin' things, aren't you, Kev, not Black Nat?"

"No, 'course not!" he lied. "What do you think I am?"

"Crazy!" Ben fumed. "I've a good mind to go and tell old Smithy.'

"Don't do that," Kevin pleaded. "All right, so I've been helping myself to a few things, but mates don't grass on each other, do they, eh? Look, you can have

some of the stuff, OK? Go shares… "

Ben swept the offered money out of Kevin's hand. "I don't need any of it, and nor do you. Why have you started doin' all this?"

Kevin saw his chance to wheedle his way out. "Don't you see?" he whined. "I'm doing it on purpose so we can get rid of her. C'mon, Ben, old pal, admit it – none of us want her sort in this school, do we?"

Ben remained unconvinced by the excuse, but couldn't quite work out what was the best thing to do. "Don't seem right to me, though, stickin' the blame on her for all this thievin'," he said vaguely.

"So what?" Kevin retorted and gabbled on in relief now that he could tell Ben was weakening. "Who cares about Black Nat? Like I said, it was all part of my plan to get her into trouble, but I promise I won't nick any more – honest! We'll grab her soon and force her to confess, right, and that'll be the end of it – and her, too, hopefully."

Ben took some further persuading, but as Natalie listened with mounting horror, she heard Ben agree to say that they'd both seen her through the windows, searching the coats. She felt sick, realising there would be no point in going to report what had happened. It'd just be her word against theirs and she knew who'd be the loser.

The way she looked at it, with no-one on her side, she hadn't a hope of winning...

For the first time at Orchard Primary, Natalie at last scented the possibility of victory. The kind of help that she'd needed before was now there, ready and willing, and Ben in goal seemed the perfect target for gaining a spot of sweet revenge!

Although he'd only ever played there in practice, Ben had been quick to volunteer to don the yellow jersey and gloves. With Kevin in disgrace, kicking Natalie no longer seemed so much fun. He badly needed a chance to think – about whether to own up too – and standing between the posts seemed the best place to be able to do it. He didn't expect to be kept very busy.

Soon, however, other worries began to cross his mind. The young sub wasn't marking Natalie tightly enough, allowing her too much space to run at him. Ben shouted a warning, but it was too late. The Millbank captain, her confidence boosted further at finding much firmer ground under her feet on this side of the pitch, was already taking the boy on at speed.

He never stood a chance.

Zipping past him easily, Natalie also flew by another lumbering defender before passing the ball inside to Darryl on the edge of the penalty area. Ben managed to block the centre-forward's well-struck shot, but fumbled the ball and finally had to kick it away in panic.

"That's the way, Flash," Darryl shouted, applauding her. "You show 'em you mean business."

This dangerous, opening attack of the second period seemed to alter the whole course of the game, driving doubts into the Orchard players' minds straight after their devastating half-time upset. Their earlier cockiness had deserted them and now even their will to win began leaking away like air from a punctured balloon.

Mr Smith knew the reason why such a change had come over the boys, but the parents on the touchline could only watch in amazement – and increasing admiration – as the black girl winger tore the home side's defence apart.

Tall and slim, Natalie had the grace of movement, in full flight, to dance and float past other players, making them look stiff and wooden by comparison. Time and again, she

tricked and teased them with her close dribbling skills, and then left them for dead with scorching bursts of acceleration, her long black hair flowing out behind like a mane.

After setting up several chances for others to miss, it was Natalie herself who levelled the match at 2–2. She found the same net as before, but this goal counted for the right team.

Not even Jonathan's wild lunge could prevent her skipping clear of the defence yet again and, as Ben raced out towards her to narrow the shooting angle, she decided to lob the ball cheekily over his head. Stranded way off his line, the keeper watched it curl high above him and then suddenly dip and drop down into the empty, gaping goal.

He sank to his knees in despair, but she had no time for gloating. She brushed away her team-mates' congratulations, retrieved the ball from the net and ran with it under her arm straight back to the centre circle for the game to be restarted without delay.

"C'mon, we've still got some work to do," she urged when they eventually caught up with her. "The match isn't over yet."

But with the visitors now so much on top and

helped further by the strong wind, the final result was open to little doubt. Soon, Millbank were ahead, Ben flapping at the ball with one hand as another of Natalie's accurate left-wing crosses swirled into his goalmouth. He only succeeded in pushing it out to the lurking Gurpreet, who reacted quickly to sidefoot it over the line.

That was about as much as Ben could stand. The next time Natalie broke free and cut into the penalty area, he saw her hesitate in the face of his advance, uncertain whether to pass or shoot. He launched himself at her like the full-back he normally was, feet-first, hacking away her legs as she unwisely tried to jink round his crude tackle.

Down she went in a heap, and up went the cry of "Penalty!" from the rest of the Millbank team. The referee had no choice but to point to the spot.

As Natalie began to limp away to let Darryl take the penalty as usual, he tossed the ball into her arms. "Captain's job," he grinned. "And that's you today, Flash. It's all yours. Have fun."

Natalie had no experience of taking a penalty, not even in training, but she could not resist one last chance to outwit Ben. As for the goalkeeper, he almost felt like handing over the gloves to someone else to escape further humiliation. Then, resigning himself to his fate, he crouched on the line, ready to spring.

Praying he might perhaps salvage a little self-respect by saving her penalty, Ben dived to the right as she shaped to strike the ball. His guess was a good one. That was the way Natalie had intended it to go, but unfortunately for him, she miskicked. As he sprawled in the mud near the post, the ball looped to his left and bobbled into the opposite corner of the goal.

After being mobbed by her delighted team-mates, Natalie noticed Ben was still lying miserably on the ground and went over to offer him a helping hand back up. Taken by surprise, he accepted.

"Only just," he muttered.

"Was a bit lucky," she conceded with a smile and then pretended to tap a few buttons on a calculator, reminding him of his previous jibe. "But that makes the score 4–2 to us now, I reckon."

"OK, OK," he said, giving a heavy sigh. "Guess I deserve that. You win, Black Nat…

sorry, I mean, you win, Flash!"

When the final whistle blew, both Natalie and Jonathan led their teams in cheering for the opposition, and she was amazed how many of the Orchard boys came up to shake her hand before they left the field.

"Well played! You were incredible second half, Flash," Jonathan was big enough to say, using her nickname himself in the hope of making up. "Pity you weren't playing for us instead, that's all."

"Would you have let me?" she asked.

"Now, you bet, but don't suppose we would last year," he admitted, shame-faced. "Really sorry, we are, about everything. Kevin gave himself away at half-time. He was the one doing all that stealing."

"I know, I saw him once."

Jonathan was shocked. "What, and you never said anything?"

"Would only have made things worse," she replied with a shrug before looking Ben straight in the eye. "But you knew the truth, didn't you?"

He nodded, avoiding his captain's hard stare. "Yeah, but I mean, you can't go rattin' on your mates, can yer?"

"Sometimes friends have to tell each other what they're doing is wrong," Natalie said, surprising herself. "Anyway, now he'll find out who his real friends are, won't he?"

"What d'yer mean?" Ben asked, puzzled, but the question was answered for her.

"She means," Jonathan stressed, "that now Kev's in big trouble, it's up to us to stand by him and tell Smithy what we did, too. Not let him take all the blame himself. Right, Flash?"

"Yeah, something like that," she grinned. "Maybe me coming back here today has turned out right after all – even for Kevin in the end!"

Back in the cloakroom, once the scene of her nightmares, Natalie found herself surrounded again. But this time, only so that Mr Smith could apologise to her in front of everyone for things that had happened in the past.

"If ever anybody had a score to settle with us, then it was you today, Natalie," he finished. "And you certainly did so – twice!"

"Three times, if you count my own goal," she put in.

"Exactly," the teacher said and then produced a muddy leather football from behind his back

to give her. "Something more pleasant to remember Orchard Primary School by, I hope. This is the match ball for you to keep to celebrate your hat-trick!"

When the laughter had died down, Natalie had a chance to say her thanks before holding the ball up over her head like a trophy for all the boys to see.

"Just so that nobody thinks I've gone and pinched it," she explained, smiling mischievously.